Dewdrop Babies

The Summer Party

Patricia MacCarthy

PICTURE CORGI

The Dewdrop Babies are very excited.
Today it's their summer party, and all
their friends are invited.

Now it's time to get everything ready!

Bluebell and Sweetpea are
in charge of the decorations.

Spider has been weaving silken thread all week, and
the ballroom is strewn with shimmery silk garlands.

Violet is planning the party entertainment, with help from Waterlily. The ants are practising their acrobatics,

the dragonflies are zooming and diving,
ready for their flying display,

and all the animals are trying out their acts.

Buttercup, Poppy and Rose are in the palace kitchen preparing the feast.

They have made
little seed parcels

and roasted nut snacks,

wild strawberries set on
sugared rose petals,

and elderflower cordial
served in acorn cups.

And now they are each making
something secret . . .

"I'm making the most beautiful cake ever."

They measure and mix, grind
and blend, crash and bang.

"My cake will be perfect!"

"My cake will be amazing!"

Then they pop their cakes into the ovens.

They are hot and bothered
after all their hard work.

Suddenly they see a plume of smoke . . .

"Oh no! My cake is burnt!"
cries Buttercup.

"Mine is all runny,"
sighs Poppy.

"I forgot to put honey in
mine," moans Rose. "It was
meant to be a honey cake!"

Violet runs into the kitchen to find three very
cross Dewdrop Babies and three ruined cakes!
"Why have you made three? We only need one!"

Then they all burst out laughing.

And instead of getting hot and bothered . . .

they decide to work together . . .

. . . and make the best cake ever.

"It's not runny."

"It's not burnt."

"And it's full of honey!"

Now the feast is ready, the palace is sparkling,

the grasshoppers are chirruping,

and it's party time!

The entertainment begins and the
whole palace is filled with laughter.

And everyone agrees that Buttercup, Poppy and Rose really did make the best cake ever – together, thanks to Violet!

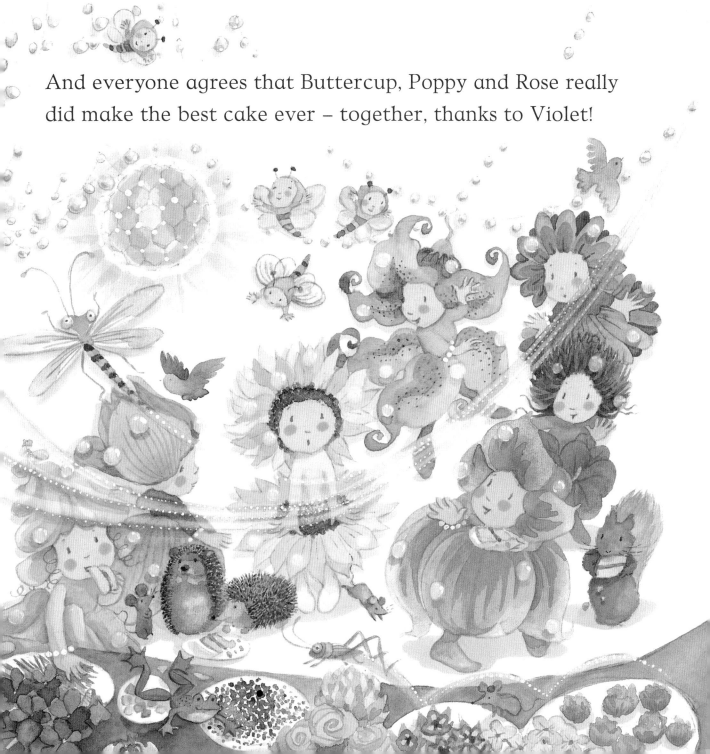

For Lydia, Bethan and Rhys

THE SUMMER PARTY

A PICTURE CORGI BOOK 978 0 552 57595 9

First published in Great Britain by Picture Corgi,
an imprint of Random House Children's Books
A Random House Group Company

This edition published 2008

3 5 7 9 10 8 6 4 2

Picture Corgi Books are published by Random House Children's Books,
61-63 Uxbridge Road, London W5 5SA

www.dewdropbabies.com
www.rbooks.co.uk

Addresses for companies within The Random House Group Limited can be found
at: www.randomhouse.co.uk/offices.htm

THE RANDOM HOUSE GROUP Limited Reg. No. 954009

A CIP catalogue record for this book is available from the British Library.

Printed in China